SMOKEHOUSE FIVE

PLATINUM
EDITIONS

SMOKEHOUSE FIVE
by Sergio Aragones

Book One
Colored by
VERA GLUMAC-PRLESI

Published by
PLATINUM EDITIONS
5321 Sterling Center Drive
Westlake Village, California 91361-4613
Phone: 818/889-9800
Fax: 818/889-6800

ISBN 1-56398-024-X

Copyright © 1991 Sergio Aragonés and Strip Art Features.
All rights reserved.
No part of this publication may be printed or reproduced
in any form or by any means without the written permission
of the publisher.

PLATINUM EDITIONS is trademark of
SAF B.V. and Malibu Graphics Publishing Group.

SCOTT ROSENBERG
President Malibu

ERVIN RUSTEMAGIĆ
President SAF

DAVE OLBRICH
Publisher

CHRIS ULM
Editor-In-Chief

TOM MASON
Creative Director

DUŠKO DIMITROV
Art Director

RADMILA ZUBAC
Production Manager

CHRISTINE HSU
Controller

5

6

7

10

9

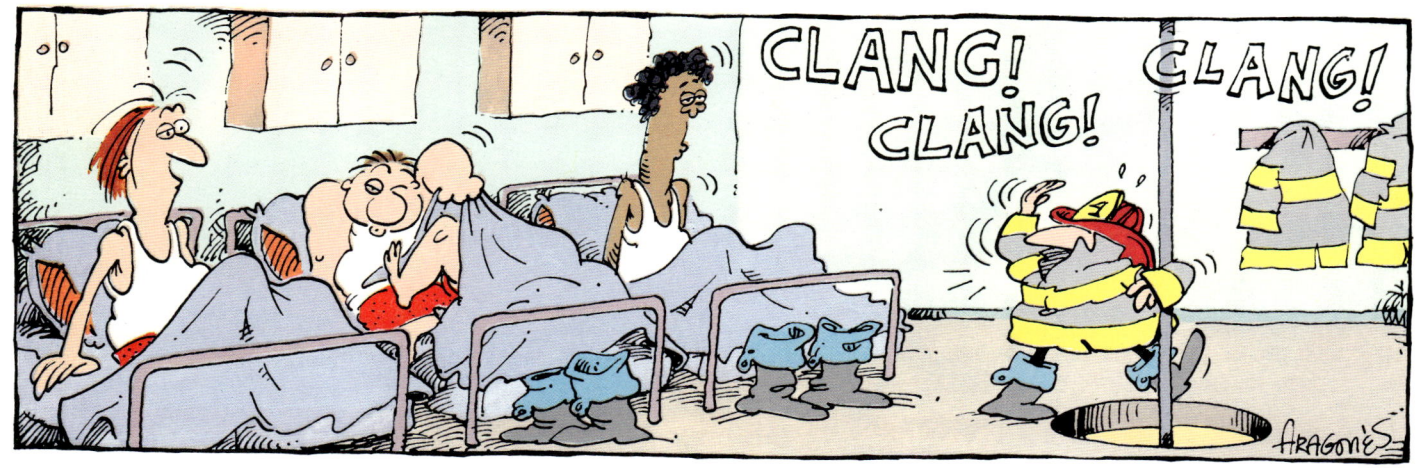

13

14

15

17

20

22

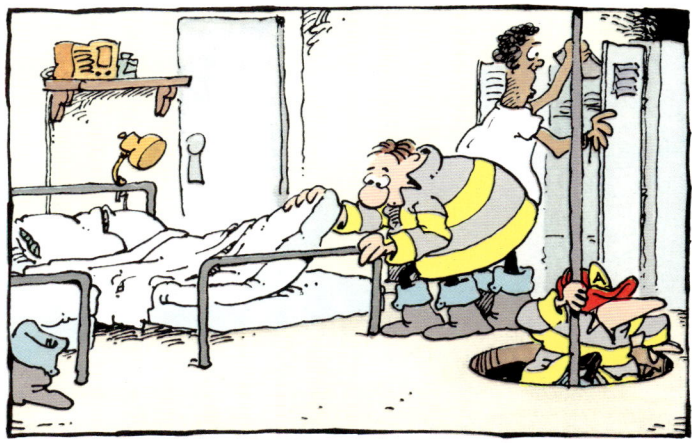

21

22

24

GUARD DOGS

24

THUNK!
CLANK!
PLUNK!

25

ARAGONES

26

28

28

29

30

ARAGONES

33

34

36

36

ARAGONÉS

Born in Spain in 1937, Sergio Aragonés emigrated to Mexico with his family where he grew up to be a cartoonist. His career really took off after he moved to New York and began working for *Mad Magazine* (and has been with them ever since).

Sergio entered the U. S. comic book field in 1967, producing stories and gags for D. C. Comics' *House Of Mystery, Plop* and *Bat Lash* series. But it was not until the mega-success of *Groo The Wanderer* that his comic book work began appearing monthly. *Groo* is published monthly by the Epic division of *Marvel Comics.*

Sergio's two newest comic creations are *Buzz & Bell* and *Smokehouse Five,* the antics of one of the least competent teams of firefighters in the world. Both *Buzz & Bell* and *Smokehouse Five* have become hugely popular around the world since their introduction in 1990, having been published by Dupuis in France, Belgium and Holland, El Pais in Spain, Totem in Italy, Williams and Carlsen in Germany, Aftonbladet in Sweden, Semic in Norway and Finland, Jik Jang In in Korea, Utusan Melayu in Malaysia, Living Media in India, Mashehu in Israel, etc.

DENDROS
PRINTERS OF COMICS ZELHEM-HOLLAND